LITTLE MISS TIDY

by Roger Hargreaves

Grosset & Dunlap

Little Miss Tidy was an extraordinarily tidy person.

In Little Miss Tidy's house everything had its place.

She had a huge handbag.

Which she would fill with all sorts of things until she had time to put them away tidily.

Then there were all her boxes.

She had small ones,
medium-sized ones,
big ones,
enormous ones,
round ones,
and square ones.

And this was where Little Miss Tidy tidied away all her things.

Nothing was ever left lying around in her house.

Now, with all this tidying up going on you would think that Little Miss Tidy was perfect, wouldn't you?

Well, she isn't!

On Monday at nine o'clock, she telephoned Mr. Clever.

"As you are so clever," she said, "could you tell me where I put my hairbrush when I tidied up?"

On Tuesday at ten o'clock, she telephoned Mr. Stingy.

"As you like money so much," she said, "could you tell me where I put my purse when I tidied up?"

On Wednesday at eleven o'clock, she telephoned Mr. Strong.

"As you like eggs so much," she said, "could you tell me where I put my boiled egg when I tidied up?"

On Thursday at twelve o'clock, she telephoned Mr. Nosey.

"As you are always poking your nose into things," she said, "could you tell me where I put my serving spoon when I tidied up?"

On Friday, she didn't telephone anybody because she had tidied away her telephone and she had to run all the way to Little Miss Chatterbox's house.

"As you love using the telephone," she said, "could you tell me where I put my telephone when I tidied up?"

Luckily, thanks to her friends, Little Miss Tidy was able to find all the things she had lost that week.

Her hairbrush was in a glove box.

Her purse was in a shoe box.

Her boiled egg was in the salt container.

Her serving spoon was in the toolbox.

And her telephone was in her sewing basket.

Little Miss Tidy certainly was very absentminded when it came to remembering where she had put things when she was tidying up.

But she couldn't help it.

On Saturday, it was her birthday and Little Miss Chatterbox came to her house, carrying a splendid-looking box all tied up with red ribbon.

Little Miss Tidy couldn't wait to see what was inside the present.

It was a notebook and pencil.

The perfect present for somebody who lost things as easily as Little Miss Tidy.

Little Miss Tidy was as happy as . . . well, as happy as Mr. Happy!

She spent the rest of the day opening all her boxes and writing down in her notebook everything that she had stored away in them.

It was very late by the time she finished her list.

She went to bed, very tired.

On Sunday morning, she woke with a start.

"My notebook and pencil!" she cried.

"Wherever did I put them when I tidied up?"

Little Miss Tidy spent all day Sunday looking for her notebook and pencil.

She had to open and close all her boxes again.

And do you know where she eventually found her notebook and pencil?

On her bedside table!